A Mook For All Time

By: Duane F Coyle

A Cold Beginning

Sitting in one's underwear in a field during winter has a way of creating a unique perspective of one's life. Simply put, mine sucks.

You may be asking yourself, 'Why is this idiot frosting his jewels instead of enjoying a hot mug of cocoa while watching the latest flick on the big screen?' Simple. I am out of cocoa, there is nothing on T.V., and the general population knows nothing about electricity, let alone who Jeff Probst is.

You see, just a few days ago, my friend and I were enjoying such times. Now we get to enjoy running from demons, hiding from vicious creatures, and bar wenches. O.K., so maybe it isn't all bad. Basically, we're traded the vile IRS for the not so vile fire breathing dragon.

If you think this is confusing, wait until you see you're next tax refund. To ease you into the story, let me explain how we got to this field.

Chapter 1

The Postman and the Book

In which we get some mail, find some peef, puff smoke, and

stand in a pigsty.

Vinny and I have been friends for years. We were roommates in college, dated a few of the same girls, and even started a band called Mook. Now we share a small apartment in the suburbs. Being typical males, we weren't even sure what color carpet we had. We just knew that under the dirty clothes, pizza boxes, and magazines lived the carpet.

Today was a typical day. Vinny and I were watching the latest Sam Raimi movie, 'Evil Dead Part 6', and drinking some cocoa. We were just getting into a great debate on if Bruce Campbell could beat up Spiderman when the doorbell rang, twice. This may not seem odd, but we didn't have a doorbell.

Vinny opened the door to reveal a short, jolly-looking fat man in a red coat trimmed in white. He had on thick glasses and a postal hat.

"You're early," commented Vinny.

"Nope," replied the jolly old man, "November 26th,

three forty-five P.M., right on time. Are you Mr.

Machia…..?"

"Vincenzo Macavinni?" Vinny asked.

"That's it," the postman said, looking quite relieved.

"This is for you."

With that, he handed Vinny a package, gave a nod, laid

a finger beside his nose, and walked away. Vinny shut the

door and sat down. After looking at the package for a

minute he looked up at me.

"What do ya think it is?"

I shrugged, "It's got your name on it, doesn't it?"

"Naw, there isn't any name on it, it's completely

blank," Vinny replied.

Vinny shrugged and ripped the plain brown paper off

and held up his prize, a plain brown box. He looked like a

little kid on Christmas morning. "It's a box!" Vinny

exclaimed."

"Hey Vinny, open the box." I coaxed.

He blushed a bit and popped the end open. Inside was a

leather-bound book. He flipped it over a few times as if

he'd never seen one before.

"What's wrong, forgot how to read?" I asked.

"Look at the title." He replied.

He passed over the book and I looked at the title. It

was 'Time Travel for Dummies'.

"Looks like someone knows what you like, Vinny."

"Do you think it's real?" He asked, ignoring my previous comment.

"You mean, do I think a dummy could travel through time? You go first."

Vinny opened the book, scanned through the prologue, passed the chapter on physics, and stopped on chapter four.

Chapter 4

To time travel, one must get all the ingredients mixed into a large bowl. Then speak the incantation, and perform the gesture. When the smoke clears, you will have arrived n your destination.

Ingredients:

Lilac scented candle wax

Peef

An item from where you want to go

One (1) toe from a Butterfly

Bring the items to a boil, speak the words:

"Veratas Nicto" and blow a kiss to your current time and place.

"Let's try it!" Exclaimed Vinny. He had the look of a kid at Toys R Us during a going out of business sale.

"Why would we want to leave the here and now? Besides,

we don't have any of the stuff needed." I replied.

"I have the candle wax. It's under the sink in the bathroom."

"You have a candle? Why is it under the bathroom sink?" I asked, very curious, but at the same time, not wanting to know the answer.

Vinny grinned at me. "Smells better than the alternative." I groaned, visual images nauseating me.

"O.K., so how about peef?" I asked.

"One sec," he replied and disappeared into his room. A moment later he returned with a jar of swirling brown liquid.

"What is peef?" I asked.

"You don't want to know, dude." He answered. I believed him; after all, it did come from his bedroom.

"So how about a toe from a Butterfly. Last time I checked they don't have toes." I asked smugly, knowing this one would stop this nonsense.

Vinny chuckled, "My Butterfly does, but I don't know if a gerbil would count."

This time I disappeared into his room. That is one trip that will haunt me for the rest of my life. I returned a couple minutes later, a small white toe in my hand.

"You didn't kill my gerbil, did you? You sick bas..."

"Whoa Vinny," I cut him off, "the gerbil was already dead. It looks like it suffocated. That probably happened days ago by the look of things."

"That explains why she wouldn't eat her antipasto last night," Vinny replied nodding.

I added the toe to the pot Vinny got from the kitchen. The kitchen was the cleanest room in the house. After all, why mar great Italian food by cooking it in a dirty kitchen. It's like making love in a Ford Pinto, you just don't do it.

"Guido, where do you wanna go to? We still need the item from another time."

My mind started spinning. What do I have in my collection of oddities that represents a time I want to visit? My original sheet music of 'Tuxedo Junction'? Or maybe my signed photo of Charlie Chaplin. Maybe even my prehistoric plant fossil.

"Dude, how about this?" Vinny held up a lock of dark hair fixed with a ribbon. A note attached to the ribbon read "Come to me". The writing was elegant, obviously feminine.

I shrugged. A woman's hair bears getting eaten by a raptor any day. Vinny dropped the hair in with the rest of the ingredients'. The mixture bubbled and popped, a foul-smelling purple smoke started to rise from it. Together we spoke the words and blew a kiss, Vinny to his bedroom, me to my computer.

Green smoke turned to orange as it billowed from the pot. I couldn't see anything, not that it mattered much. The smell of burning ravioli assailed my nose. The sounds of hysterical laughter set my nerves on end. Finally, the smoke cleared, the smell changed to that of mud, and Vinny continued to laugh.

"That stuff is great! What a buzz!" he laughed.

"I think we did it, Vinny," I said in amazement.

Our apartment had been replaced with mud, muck, and a pig. Our best friends would never notice the difference.

Vinny stopped laughing, looked around, and pointed to the pig.

"Look, a medieval pig!" he exclaimed.

"Yeah Vinny, and a medieval farmer with a very medieval-looking crossbow." I cautioned staring at the farmer not moving.

"Do you think he wants to get medieval on your ass?" Vinny asked, barely controlling his laughter.

I glared at him, raised my hands, and said the first thing I could think of to the armed farmer.

"We come in peace."

Chapter 2

Were are We?

In which we meet a farmer, a pig, and a kitty, and get

propositioned by one of them.

"What are ya doin' in ma pigsty and what are ya doin' wit

ma son? The farmer asked, pointing the crossbow right at my

head.

"We, um..." offered Vinny.

"What my friend is trying to say is, we just kinda

fell in." I offered, not taking my eyes off the arrow

cocked and ready to end my travels.

"What son, all I see is this pig?" asked Vinny, not

caring about the weapon pointed at me.

"My son, he's wereswine." The farmer said, using the

crossbow to gesture to the pig trying to eat Vinny's shirt.

"I don't know where your son is!" yelled Vinny getting

upset, "And don't call me a swine."

The farmer's grip tightened on the trigger. Just when

I was wondering how my body would compare to a pincushion,

a strange sound cut the tension. The pig next to us started

to jerk, its skin bubbling. With a smell not unlike

overcooked bacon, it morphed into an eleven-year-old boy.

Okay, so an eleven-year-old boy wearing a pig costume.

"Git away from ma boy!" the farmer shouted, aiming the crossbow.

"Poppa, wait!" yelled a voice from behind us. I glanced back and was startled by the sight. Where the farmer was dirty, rail-thin, and about as ugly as the Federal Budget, his daughter was anything but. She had cascading dark red hair that darkened to black near the ends. She moved with a fluid grace that sent chills through me. Her piercing green eyes shone brightly against her lightly tanned skin.

"Poppa, I think these are the ones sent to help us. Look at their strange clothes." She said to him as she put a hand on the crossbow, moving it so my head was not the target anymore. I let out the breath I was startled to find out I was holding.

Now Vinny and I pride ourselves on how we dress. That is to say, I am proud of my clothes, typically a black dress shirt, silver tie, and black leather pants. Vinny is proud to just be able to dress himself. Today he was wearing his pink Hawaiian shirt, ripped jeans, and sandals.

"The prophecy said that a person from the future would come to save us. You are from the future, correct?" asked the girl, with a pleading, desperate look in her mesmerizing eyes.

"We're from Florence," Vinny said very proudly.

"Italy?" she asked.

"Nope, South Carolina," Vinny corrected.

"So ya sayin they is from da future?" the farmer asked his daughter. I had forgotten he was there.

She smiled and nodded. I scanned the barn for an exit. Vinny grinned.

"Got anything to eat? I'm starved."

Leave it to Vinny to make a great impression. Where we should be heading for the hills to escape these nuts, Vinny is looking for grub.

The farmer finished lowering his crossbow, took his pig-son by the hand, and led him to the farmhouse. The enchanting girl turned to us.

"Come with me, you can wash up and join us for dinner. I'll explain everything to you then."

"Hey, what's your name?" I called to her as she turned.

"Oh! I have lost my manners! My name is Kitty." She blushed and turned to follow her father into the house.

"Kitty" I whispered. The name fit her fluid movements. I realized Vinny was staring at me with that stupid grin on his face. I punched him in the arm and gestured for him to follow Kitty.

We followed her into a rundown log house. A fire crackled, warming us. The smell of freshly baked bread hung in the air. Kitty pointed to the sink.

"You can wash up there; join us in the next room when you're done." She sauntered through the partition.

We washed up in the ice-cold water and entered the dining room. The room was barely big enough for the five of us, but we all managed to gather at the large oak table. Several covered dishes were set out.

"Please, dig in." offered Kitty.

The lids came off revealing a dozen plates with various fruits and vegetables. There were apples, pears, potatoes, cabbages, snap peas, corn, and steaming fresh bread. They were all raw, except for the bread.

"Um, isn't anything cooked?" asked Vinny.

"Why would it be? That would be unnatural." Kitty replied with a puzzled look on her beautiful face.

Vinny shrugged, "Got any steaks?"

The farmer blanched, staring at Vinny.

"I'm sorry Mr.…" Kitty began.

"Vincenzo Macavinni. My friends and all of them pretty girls call me Vinny. The really hot chicks call me Vinny the Mac. What would you call me?" he asked as he flashed her that stupid grin that the girls just eat up.

"Incorrigible," I interjected to save him from himself.

Kitty flashed me a grateful smile. Strange, her smiles made me want to leap over the table and pounce on her. "And what is your name?" she said to me.

"Guido."

"That's it, only one name?"

"Just Guido, kinda like Madonna, Cher, or Teller. One name sums me up." I replied.

"Yeah, but that one name isn't polite in mixed company." Vinny shot back with pear juice dripping down his chin.

I shot Vinny an evil look. The last thing I wanted was a beauty like Kitty thinking I'm some kind of womanizer. Yeah, I was, but I didn't want her to know that.

"As I was saying," she continued, "we do not eat meat here, especially that of cow or pig." With that, she gestured towards her brother, who was noisily chewing on a corn cob.

"What's wrong with him, anyway?" I asked.

"He is were, a lycanthrope. All of us are. You are in the town of Lycan, a town completely populated by werecreatures. For instance," she continued to explain when she noticed the puzzled expression on my face. "I am a werecat. My natural state is that of a Persian feline. My father is a werecow, and as you know, my brother is a wereswine. For two seasons a year, we turn into human form to grow crops, build shelters, and mate. The rest of the time we spend it in our natural animal forms."

"But your brother..." I began.

"We all can change at will to either form; it is just simpler to tolerate our winters as an animal. In fact, we are but mere weeks until the next phase." She interrupted me.

Vinny grinned, I really hate it when he does that.

"I get it, you become a kitty, so your name is Kitty. Is your brother named Piggy?" Vinny choked out, barely controlling his laughter.

I kicked him under the table, shoving an apple into his mouth as he cried out. "Forgive my friend, he was raised by chimps."

"What a coincidence," exclaimed Kitty, "Our neighbors are werechimps! You may be related!"

Vinny burst out laughing, nearly choking on his apple.

"You said that we are here to help. What is it that you need?" I asked her, trying to get the conversation back on track.

"Our village has been plagued by the evil Count Siva. His murderous ways have led to the disappearance of several of our residents, including my own mother." Kitty explained.

"What were is she?" Vinny asked.

"She was a werechicken," replied the farmer as he wiped the tears from his dirty cheeks.

"Does that mean you were henpecked?" asked Vinny with a straight face.

"VINNY SHUT UP!" I shouted at him. I couldn't believe he'd just said that.

"We don't have much to offer in payment." Kitty continued, ignoring Vinny's last comment. "We can give you food, a place to sleep, and anything you want to take from Count Siva's castle after he is destroyed."

"Sounds like a deal, but tell us, why don't you all just confront him? And why destroy him, why not just have your police arrest him and try him for murder." I asked.

"Because," Kitty said, "Count Siva is a vampire."

Chapter 3

Vampires 101

In which Vinny reads a book and buys a map to nowhere.

The next morning we found ourselves incredibly hungry and nervous about our quest.

"What do you mean you don't have the book?" I yelled at Vinny. "How are we supposed to get home?"

"Relax, man. Kitty said last night that we'd have to search the library for vampire information. We can look for another time travel book there." Vinny said not sounding concerned that we could be stuck here for good at all.

"You do realize that this culture has yet to invent indoor toilets. What makes you think they would have a book on time travel?" I asked.

"If this place has vampires, it can travel in time." He replied confidently.

We walked across town amid glares and growls. Several people could be seen peeking through the windows. When we finally reached the library we were amazed to find a large brick building. Clearly, it was a place of pride. The white bricks looked recently washed. The windows were of expensive stained lead glass.

The interior was even more impressive. Pillars of glass reached from floor to ceiling every fifteen feet. Each one channeled light, leaving no corner darkened. Rows of books stretched as far as I could see, with the shelves reaching a full twenty feet to the ceiling above. Incredibly there were dozens of large birds, owls mostly with some eagles also. These birds were flying from readers to shelves, sorting books, replacing them, and retrieving books from the highest and farthest reaches.

A gentleman in midnight blue approached us, a large falcon on his wrist.

"Good morning gentlemen, and welcome to the Lycan Center of Learning. We have the world's largest assortment of books and scrolls ever collected. How can we assist you?"

"An umbrella would be nice," commented Vinny.

"What we need is assistance on books about vampires," I said.

"Very good sir, Colleen would be happy to help." With that, the falcon hopped off the man's wrist and quickly changed into a woman in her early twenties. Much like her bird self, she had jet black hair and sparkling eyes.

"I can take care of these two, professor." Said the raven-haired Colleen.

The professor bowed to us and walked off. I glanced at Vinny, jabbed him with my elbow, and finally stepped in front of Vinny to break his stare.

"What we require is a book about vampires. Maybe anything written concerning Count Siva." I began.

Colleen morphed back into a raven, breaking Vinny's trance, and flew off.

"Vinny, what do you know about vampires?" I asked.

"History states that the vampire is an undead creature that feeds off the living. Several 'rules' have been placed by various authors. Some say a vampire must be invited to enter a home. A stake through the heart can destroy them. They hate garlic and love rock music."

I was about to comment on Vinny's apparent clarity of mind and speech when he added at the last second, "Dude". Sometimes I wonder if his stoned, burnt out appearance is just an act.

"So basically we offer him some good Italian cooking, heavy on the garlic, and stake him when he chokes."

Vinny shrugged, "Either that or expose him to sunlight."

Colleen returned with the first book, dropped it on the table, and then flew off. The book was History of Lycan, Count Siva was the author. According to the dust cover, Lycan was a village that was ravaged by war, evil spirits, and demons. It was finally wiped out by one man after a century of peace. The picture on the back was of a graying man in a black tuxedo.

Then it hit me, a dust jacket and press photo? Colleen landed with the second book, I quickly waved to her.

"Colleen, what year is it?"

She flew off, leaving me unsure if she even heard me. Vinny gave me a puzzled look. I pointed to the photo.

"Since when did the dark ages have Eastman Kodak photography?"

Vinny grabbed the book, opened it, and gasped.

"Guido, this book was published in 1992."

I picked up the second book. This one was the classic 'Dracula' as published in 1898.

"Vinny, how could this library have books from the future?"

"Government spending." He replied. I ignored him.

"Vinny, are you thinking what I am thinking?"

"How ironic is it that two beavers can hold up a mini-mart armed only with a burrito?" He asked.

I stared at him for a moment, not sure I even wanted to know where that came from. "No, you idiot. I think the book that sent us here is from this library."

He gave me his best 'ya think?' look and began doodling on some scrap paper. Colleen flew up with another book, this one about vampire sightings at twenty-first-century colleges.

"Colleen, wait." I quickly said. She paused for a moment, "Do you have the book titled 'Time Travel for Dummies'?"

She shifted back into human form, much to Vinny's pleasure, and appeared to think for a moment. "I'm sorry guys, that book is currently checked out."

"To whom?" I almost shouted.

"Sorry, that information is private." She answered.

I nodded and gathered up our books. I thanked her for her help, gathered Vinny, and made for the exit.

"Gentleman, one moment, please," came a voice from behind me. It was the professor, "You must sign out those books before you leave."

I blushed, embarrassed for forgetting. "How do we sign up?"

"The rules are simple, you place your crops as collateral until the books are returned."

"We don't have any crops," replied Vinny.

"We also accept gold."

"How about Diner's Club?" asked Vinny.

"I'll hold the books until you have sufficient funds for us to hold. Good day, gentlemen."

Dejected and bookless, we left the library. While pondering what to do next
I noticed several people staring at us again. This time I understood. We needed new clothes to fit in.

"Hey, Vinny, let's duck in here and get some new attire. IF we ever expect to figure out what's going on, we need to fit in."

Vinny nodded, either in the agreement or to the voices in his head, and followed me into what looked like a clothing store.

"Welcome sirs," greeted a smarmy-looking salesman, "how can I help you?"

"We need to make some purchases," I replied, "but we have no local currency. Is there something we can barter with?"

He eyes us over, stopping on Vinny's cubic zirconium pinky ring. It was a gift from a mutual friend of ours, named Gino Z. Gino was the owner of a nightclub where Vinny played poker.

"That diamond, it's amazing."

"That thing," I started, "but that just-"

"Perfect," stated Vinny, giving me an evil look. He

slipped off the ring and handed it to the salesman.

"Anything you gentleman want is yours. I'll trade you an entire shopping day for this ring. It must be at least five carats."

The salesman left for the back, Vinny and I split up and agreed to meet outside in twenty minutes. I was done in half that, having purchased not only an entirely new set of clothes but two blanket rolls, an extra set of boots, and a heavy coat. All in the gray to black category. Vinny didn't have the same luck, at least I hope he didn't consider it lucky.

Vinny came out sporting a white shirt, purple jacket, purple pants, a purple hat with a white feather attached, and a gold cane.

I could almost hear the 'Wakka Wah' song in my head.

"Where did you get that?

"It ain't easy." He replied.

"What ain't easy?" I asked.

He just grinned at me. I shook my head, "So what's next." I asked.

He reached into his jacket and withdrew a scroll. He opened it up, holding it in front of him, and pointed. "We go here."

"Okay, question number one, where is 'here?' Question

Chapter 4

Cheshire

In which we experience stakes of many natures.

Our trip from Lycan to Cheshire was fairly uneventful. Several times we were approached by fellow travelers, many of who quickly departed upon seeing Vinny's attire. One whispered into Vinny's ear. Curiously Vinny pointed towards me. The man shook his head and left. I meant to ask Vinny what that was about when we arrived in Cheshire.

Cheshire is a large walled city, bustling with activity and full of normal-looking people. There were no guards at the gate so we walked right in. We appeared to be in the commercial district as all we saw were stores.

"So what now?" I asked

Vinny wrinkled his nose. "Smells like someone is burning dinner."

I shrugged, "Where do we start?" I coaxed Vinny.

"Well," Vinny began, "we know will need a stake to kill the vampire. We could ask around a bit."

"You mean, walk up to a vendor and ask 'do you have anything that would kill a bloodsucking vampire?'" I joked.

number two, where did you get that?”

"I got this map from the library. While you were chatting with the professor, I lifted this from the display case. You have your talents, and I have mine."

“Okay, so where are we supposed to go?” I asked.

"I asked the salesman where to get stakes, he became excited and said the best is found in Cheshire. It's only about a day's walk from here." He answered.

“Good job, Vinny. For once your ideas are paying off.” I commented.

Vinny grinned. "How bout that place, Guido?"

Before I could stop him, Vinny walked into a nearby bar. The place was packed with people and creatures of all types. One creature bumped into me on his way out. I would have said something but his friend moved him out the door. That and he was covered in green scales, a fang-filled grin, and an evil expression. His friend seemed normal enough. He wore nondescript clothes and curly red hair. It was the dragon that threw me. I hadn't really thought about the kinds of critters we might see. But a dragon beats all, even if they are only the size of a small horse.

I saw Vinny talking to the barkeep so I wandered over. Vinny turned to me and smiled.

"What's up?" I asked.

"He said the best place for stakes is the Rosary. But they can be expensive." Vinny replied.

"So why not use your other ring, the one with the pink ice in it. You can tell them it's another diamond." I told him.

"Won't work, dude. I tried that but he just laughed at me. Somehow he knew it wasn't real" Vinny answered.

"So how do you propose we get enough money to buy a decent stake?"

Vinny reached into his purple jacket and withdrew a

deck of cards. Vinny is a poker fanatic. I estimate that he has learned nearly twenty different ways to play. At home, he obsessed about it to the point of watching it on TV.

"And what will you use for betting, we have no cash." I reminded him.

"Leave that to me," said Vinny.

Vincent Macavinni may be bad about many things, but finding poker buddies isn't one of them. Before long he had three of the roughest goons gathered at the table as he explained the ins and outs of Texas hold-em and five-card draw.

The first guy was a twig with limbs, literally. He had a grayish bark and small beady eyes. He didn't look particularly mean or tough, but there was a certain deadliness about him.

The second looked human enough, as he was roughly six feet tall and had the necessary number of fingers and toes. Truth to tell, he kinds of reminded me of Vinny's uncle Vito, or maybe it was his Aunt Trella. Both were scary looking knuckle draggers.

The third and last guy was small and wiry. He had the look of either an accountant or a tax consultant. Either one scares me like nothing else. After all, to me, it takes a sick individual to take pleasure in taking money from honest folks. Although I do have to admit the female variety of said professions are both deadly and attractive to me. Traits I kinda like.

After a few minutes of explaining the game and how to bet, Vinny waived down a passing waitress and recruited her as the dealer. He then waved me over.

"Guido, one small problem. The only way they'll play is if we have something to bet with. I kinda told them that your clothes would be the barter." Vinny said sheepishly.

"Vinny, are you out of your freakin' mind? Do you really expect me to give away my clothes? Use your own." I answered.

"I tried, dude. They won't have it. But don't worry, don't I always win." He answered.

He had me there, I've never seen anyone as lucky with cards. Before I knew it I had nodded in agreement and the game started.

"Okay gents, the game is five-card stud, chase the wench," Vinny stated.

Two of the players looked at the waitress/dealer in confusion. She simply shrugged and dealt the first three cards, two face down, one up.

"Key is, whatever card drops face up after a queen is dealt becomes the wild card. All previous wild cards become regular face value." Vinny explained.

Stick got the first card, a jack of hearts. Goon was dealt a five of spades, and Tax got a nine of diamonds. Vinny was dealt a two of diamonds. Stick tossed in a gold nugget. "My first bet will be the boots," Vinny stated.

Dutifully I pulled off my boots and set them on the table. Coins and stones of different colors followed.

After the bets stopped the second card was dealt. Stick got another jack, the club this time. Goon got a six of spades; Tax got a king of diamonds. Vinny was dealt another two, this one a heart. "Gents, let's end this quickly," Vinny said.

Stick added another nugget, this one the size of my fist. Bets followed until it was Vinny's turn. "I bet the shirt and the bedroll." He said.

As I could see that Vinny's hole card contained another two, I was confident he would win. I threw in my shirt and bedroll.

The last card was dealt. A queen of hearts dropped in front of Stick. All he had showing to win was his two jacks. Goon got his next card, a jack of diamonds. According to the rules, jacks were now wild. This meant Stick's jacks were now wild, giving him three of a kind. Tax got a four of hearts, which didn't help him any. Vinny got the last card, a king of hearts.

"Gents, I say we go all in." I tossed my pants on the table, leaving me somewhat chilly. But as I always said, I may be shy, but I am not bashful. Treasures of many forms were added to the pot.

When all was done, Vinny flipped over his hole cards, revealing his third two and second king. He had a full house. Stick flipped over his cards revealing a seven and a four, leaving him with his three of a kind. Tax shrugged and showed his ace and eight, giving him just an ace for a winning card. It was Goon who quieted the bunch. As he showed his hand I saw Vinny's smile disappear. Goon had the three, five, six, and seven of spades. His jack of diamonds was wild making it the obvious four of spades to complete a straight flush, the overall winning hand.

I stood stunned in my socks and boxers as all my possessions were passes to the Goon. Vinny looked up at me apologetically, I looked away and spotted an empty booth in the corner. The Goon followed me over and placed something in front of me. I looked up at him, hoping to reason with him.

"Tell your friend he needs to learn to pick better stooges to play with. Let him know I appreciated adding his little game to my own repertoire."

I watched him turn and leave; my clothes and bedroll with him. I picked up what he had left me. Shrugging, I unwrapped it and popped it into my mouth. As expected, it was a wintergreen breath mint. At least my breath would be minty fresh.

Vinny joined me. "Listen, Guido. Let me get another chance, I know I can win."

I cut him off with a glare. "Vin, why should you get another chance? This whole thing is your fault. You just had to play with that damned book. You just had to blow our shopping trip on clothes everyone hates. We could be home right now, watching a flick on the big screen and drinking hot cocoa with a couple of hot chicks. Instead, we were here in this bar, in the middle of nowhere while I'm wearing a pair of SpongeBob boxers and fuzzy socks."

"At least," replied Vinny. "we are inside instead of out in some field in the cold."

I was about to light into another round when the table faded out of existence. I looked up at Vinny in shock. He was staring at the patrons or lack thereof. As we watched the people and furniture all vanish. We were left standing in the bar alone, and then it too vanished.

"Looks like I spoke too soon," claimed Vinny. He was right. We were now standing in the middle of a field; all

signs of Cheshire had vanished. On top of that, it was in
the forties, in November, and I was feeling oftly drafty.

Chapter 5

Field of Dreams

In which I form a plan and get staked.

So here we are, right where I started this story. It has been a few hours since Cheshire vanished, since then I have had a lot of time to think. Vinny has used this time to curl up in his bedroll and sleep. I'm still not sure why I put up with him. Maybe I'm optimistic, I still think that one day my suspicions will be proven correct.

I was just thinking that now would be a perfect time for a reward challenge when the snapping of a twig alerted me. I had given no thought as to what creatures may roam the nights here. I was also starting to remember reading about vampires hunting at night. I quickly looked for a weapon of any sort when I saw a pair of eyes glinting in the moonlight.

"Vinny," I whispered, "wake up."

"Mommy, I said no more," mumbled Vinny, "the canned spaghetti gives me gas."

The eyes came closer, close enough for me to see what was about to devour us. It was a white Persian cat. I started to breathe easier, feeling foolish for getting so worked up. The cat walked towards me, watching me from arm's length as I crouched down.

"Here kitty, kitty, kitty. What are you doing out on a night like this?" I asked.

"Looking for you," It replied.

I jumped back quickly; stumbling over Vinny's sleeping form. The cat seemed to smile as it walked forwards, hair receding and form growing. When finished it wasn't a house cat before me, it was Kitty, the farmer's daughter.

She was dressed in a cotton blouse and a silken skirt that ruffled about her ankles. Both were the snow-white that her cat fur was. She had her hair pulled back, revealing a very tantalizing bit of neck. For a moment I envied vampires, for she had a neck worth biting.

I drew myself up, reorganized my thoughts, and privately told my hormones to go to sleep. She beckoned me over with a wave of her hand, leading me away from Vinny and over to the edge of the field. There we stood on the edge of a lake. The stars appeared to almost come alive on the moonlit water.

Kitty sat down, lightly pulling on my hand until I joined her. I shivered, not entirely from the cold. She placed her right hand on my left, which was resting on my leg. I forgot the cold air and focused on her.

"Why were you looking for us?" I asked.

"I was worried. I heard what happened at the library, so I followed your trail here."

"Wherever here is," I commented.

"You are still in Cheshire. It is only the phasing you are experiencing." She answered.

"What do you mean 'phasing'?"

"Periodically, and at random times the entire town of Cheshire phases out of existence. Those not born here are not affected." She explained.

"Wait, there were other beings, there was a guy who looked like a tree."

"He's a Klomea. They are more of this earth than many of us. In fact, I would guess he is the tree near your sleeping friend. They root at night to sleep."

"What of the dragon I saw?" I asked

"Silly, there is no such thing as dragons."

"I saw one leaving the bar," I insisted.

She giggled some more, then looked up at the stars. "Tell me," she said, "how long have you and Vinny been together?"

"By together I hope you mean friends. I would say at least ten years. We were roommates in college. I was studying music while he studied art. We dated a few of the same girls and generally grew up together. It was only fitting that we remained best friends afterward."

"I find it hard to believe he ever finished college," remarked Kitty.

"Truth to tell, he graduated top of his class. He took part in a national test of intelligence. Out of one hundred people, only two scored higher than him.

"If he is so smart, then why-" she began.

"Why is he a complete idiot?" I cut her off. "He comes off that way, mostly on purpose, I believe. I think it gives him the advantage of watching everything undetected before acting."

"Then if that is so, he would be a very valuable ally to have."

I sat there thinking a moment, feeling my anger at Vinny fade away as Cheshire had. The shiver of the night air returned to me. Sensing it, Kitty moved a bit closer, enough that I could feel the warmth radiate from her. Her arm moved around me, pulling me even closer.

I looked into her eyes, her flashing green eyes. For a moment I wondered how cold it would be to sleep on the ground alone. As her lips found mine, I knew I would stay warm till morning, maybe until noon if my luck held out.

Morning came and with it the warmth of a new day.

Cheshire had returned, the whispers of passer-byes bringing me to full attention. That and the fact that my colorful boxers were lying about five feet away. I picked them up and pulled them on. The dampness from the morning dew woke up other needs. I found the bar easily enough and luckily they knew of, and enjoyed indoor plumbing.

When I returned I wasn't surprised to find Vinny still asleep, curled up in a corner. My surprise was when I saw Goon with a deck of cards smiling at me. I walked up and joined him.

"Wanna play?" he asked.

"I have nothing to wager," I answered. Then a thought entered my morning fogged head. "I have an idea, though. You claim to be so good at cards, but I can prove to be a master. May I?"

He handed the cards to me. Many of the patrons started to watch as I shuffled the cards. I sat them down.

"Do me one favor, shuffle them up some more as I get a drink."

I stood and walked to the bar, roughly ten feet away. I ordered a drink and drew in the grit on the bar. The bartender grinned and nodded. Hoping he understood, I rejoined my card-shark friend. I picked up the cards and fanned them out.

"Pick one card, any one."

Goon pulled one out, looking at me curiously.

"Now, show everyone else, but do not tell me what it is."

He did so, still not sure of what was going on.

"Return the card to the deck and shuffle the deck. Make sure to mix them as much as you can."

This he understood. Before my eyes, the cards danced between his hands.

"Good. Now, what I will do is find your hidden card. But first, the wager. If I find the card you must give me back all my clothes, keep everything else. If I fail, you can add our servitude for one year. Agreed?"

"You don't know the card, yet you make such a wager?" He asked, astonished at my proposal.

"That's why it's called gambling," I answered flippantly.

"Agreed," Goon said.

Quickly I scooped up the cards and hurtled them at the bar. Cards flew everywhere. Several hit the barmaid as she brought me my drink. Never once did my eyes leave his.

"So where's my card?" Goon asked with a smirk.

The barmaid set my drink down. Sitting inside, surrounded by ice and water, was the ace of diamonds, his card. I smiled at him.

Twenty minutes later I was pulling my boots back on, and feeling much warmer. I walked over to a still sleeping Vinny and picked up his cane. I left the bar and followed various directions to find the store named The Rosary.

The Rosary was a fairly large store, talking up most of the block. The large double doors were open as if inviting me in. Inside I could swear I heard music from the early twentieth century. The smell of roses filled the air.

Adorning the walls were hundreds of religious symbols from as many denominations. I identified dozens of Buddha's, crosses, and pentagrams. Along one wall were mostly symbols from Hindu and Muslim cultures. Herbs were sold alongside books on numerology.

I was just enjoying the opening passages about magik when a gentleman approached. He was bigger than me, about two inches taller and a few pounds heavier. He had an innocent, child-like smile on his face. His hair was a light brown with almost a plastic-like quality. Resting on this plastic-looking mop was a papal hat with a bright yellow smiley face. He wore a name tag that read 'Hello…. My name is Mark'.

"Welcome to my shop. Welcome to The Rosary."

He quickly drew me into an embrace the quite frankly

scared me. "What can I offer you today?" he asked.

"How about ten feet of personal space?" I replied. "Actually, I'm looking for some stakes, got any?"

It almost appeared that I had said the foulest thing imaginable. There was a pure look of shock on Mark's face. Shock changed to horror. Horror then slipped away as Mark locked the door and practically dragged me to the back room.

"Look," he started, "I can get in a lot of trouble for you even saying that word. I do have some, but it will cost you."

I held up Vinny's pure gold cane. Mark looked it over and reached for it. I pulled it back. "This good enough?"

Mark nodded. I passed the cane to him.

"It looks like it was smithed in Lycan. I would say that this would be a fair trade."

He disappeared for a moment, returning with a sealed box in his hands. The box had no markings upon it.

"Keep this cold until you are ready to use them, anything else could be fatal." He warned.

I took his word and the box. I had never fought a vampire before, but I am sure they are common in a world that has lycanthropes.

"These are the finest stakes you have?" I asked, to be

sure.

"Absolutely. They come from the best sources, blessed upon arrival by myself. Just be sure not to tell anyone where you got them. The locals are funny about that." Mark cautioned me.

"Hey no problem," replied Vinny. "We understand the importance of the anonymity of the local supplier type persons. After all, who are we to let people know that you have the means to take down a real bloodsucker?"

"What do tax collectors have to do with your quest?" asked Mark.

I grabbed Vinny by the elbow as he was about to launch into a tirade about big government and overspending. No actually, I was pulling him away from a strange-looking moss-like substance growing on the counter. We beat a retreat out of the shop and headed out of town.

After walking for several hours in the base direction of the castle, we decided it was time to make camp for the night. We made our way to an inn, and after a quick poker game, Vinny was able to win enough to cover both dinner and a place to sleep in for the night. My only hope is that this place stays put for me to sleep.

We made our way up the stairs to the second floor and found our room. I felt guilty about Vinny's cane, but somehow I didn't really want to deal with it right then. We were finally ready to meet and fight Count Siva. The plan was simple, make our way into his castle during the morning hours and destroy him by nightfall.

I placed the box of stakes on the floor between us. Vinny smiled and cut through the seals with a knife. Excitement raced through me as he opened the box. The lid blocked my view but I could tell it was wondrous by Vinny's expression.

"Quick, let me see," I said excitedly.

Vinny grinned and turned the box towards me.

"You did say steaks, right?" Vinny asked with a laugh. Sure enough, the box was filled with a dozen steaks. Thick and juicy looking, ready for the fire and a bit of sauce.

"So now we walk in and offer up a t-bone?"

"No Vinny, now we try to find a way home. I quit."

I left the box and walked out of the room. At that moment I didn't care where I slept. I didn't care what happened. I had given it my best try and failed. It was only when my thoughts turned to Kitty and her family did I stop. I turned around and nearly ran over Vinny, who happened to be right behind me.

"Guido, I have an idea. Vampires can't stand garlic, right?"

I nodded.

"So let's give him the steaks, we'll ask to meet him, then feed him the laced t-bones. While he is choking on the garlic you can destroy him with a cross."

"Vinny, that just might work."

Vinny smiled like a little kid.

"So let's get some sleep, tomorrow is the big day."

I nodded in agreement. That night I had a dream that I was an alley cat chasing a pure white Persian.

Chapter 6

Evil Plans

In which we meet the Count and count on our meat.

Count Siva paced within his castle. It had been three days since his last hunt. Since then he has had to endure alternative sources of food. For the third time in as many hours, he walked his way down the halls, down the main stairway, and into the larder. As he had suspected, nothing had changed. How he longed for the days when food was plentiful.

Siva could not remember how long he had lived in this castle. He had vague memories of moving here as a child. Long years had passed before he became the man he is now. Yet memories of sumptuous meals prepared by servants threatened his hold on reality.

Tomorrow, he concluded, I will go to Lycan. Tomorrow I will take what I crave. Let no man or beast stop me.

Count Siva walked back up the stairs to his study. On the desk was a note written in elegant script. The cool night air drifted through the open window. Count Siva peered out the window and, satisfied by what he saw, drew the window shut. He walked over to his fireplace and sat on a large wrought iron chair. He opened the missive and read it quickly.

"Lord Count Siva. I have done as you have ordered. I have watched the newcomers. You have little to fear. They know nothing about your nature. They suspect nothing of me. I am merely another pretty face of distraction. They now leave Cheshire to face you. I will watch them as always."

Count Siva smiled at the news. His spy was working better than he had planned. He will have to remember to reward her for this news. But first, he must make ready for his guests. Count Siva spent the next several hours preparing his home for their arrival.

We started out early enough that we expected to reach Count Siva's home by midday. Somehow the day passed faster than we planned. When we finally reached the road that we were looking for, it was already about an hour past noon. By my figures, we still had about a two-hour hike to reach the castle.

We did learn that the box in which we carried out steaks was perpetually cold. It looked like any ordinary box, made of cardboard and sealed with gray tape. The inside, however, was always cold enough to leave a frost on anything inside. Vinny learned this the hard way, it took at least an hour to thaw out his feather for his hat.

The trip from Cheshire went smoothly, not a single person was to be seen. The only life besides ourselves was the occasional squirrel, chipmunk, or sparrow. The road passed through dense woods and finally lead us to a narrow dirt path through some rolling hills. We stopped for a late lunch of cheeses and bread. Vinny had made an attempt to purchase some form of meat but was turned down. I had to explain to him yet again that no one here eats meat.

This road through the hills was nearly barren of life. No squirrels played, no sparrows sang. Only once did we see what appeared to be a vulture circling the sun way above us. And so it went for an hour. Finally while cresting a small hill we saw a virtual oasis.

Along the road was a drink stand. It was made of stray pieces of wood nailed together with a handwritten sign that announced the products. As we approached, the stand owner popped up from behind the stand.

"VINNY," I shouted, "That's him! He's the guy who sold me the steaks!"

The man looked at me in horror.

"I don't know what you are talking about. I sell

water and wine, not steaks."

"You are him, you loon. You're Mark."

"The name isn't Mark," he replied, "Read the name tag."

The name tag said **Hello...*my name is ~~Mark~~ Ken*.**

"See!" I exclaimed, "It read Mark but you crossed it off."

Vinny pulled me to the side.

"Look, Guido, let it drop. Let's just get a drink, kill the vamp and go home."

"Say guys, how about some nice warm peef, nothing like it!"

"Peef?" I asked, "What is peef?" Before I could answer Vinny ordered two glasses of water.

"Guido, don't ask. You really don't want to know."

"Yes, I do."

I turned back to 'Ken' to ask again but was surprised to see that the booth was gone. I tried to take a drink of my water, but that had vanished also.

"Vinny was that a mirage or what. I feel so...confused."

"What mirage?" Vinny grinned at me.

"No, seriously, did I just imagine all that?"

"What booth?" Vinny started laughing.

I spent the rest of the walk trying to figure out if I even really exist.

We reached the massive doors to the castle as twilight descended. The doors opened as we stepped up. An elderly man stepped aside and waved us in.

"Good evening, gentlemen. The master awaits you in the library. Please, follow me."

We did as requested, not sure what else to do. The butler led us down a hallway filled with paintings, mostly landscapes. We ended our tour outside of the library.

"The master waits within. Good evening." He turned and left, leaving us to face his master.

The library was fairly large, containing hundreds of books. A large fireplace filled one wall, warming the room. Before the fireplace was a large velvet chair, red with black accents.

"Welcome to my home," came a voice from in the chair. A figure rose and glided towards us. I fully expected to see the classic vampire as depicted by Bram Stoker or Anne Rice. I would have even been satisfied with a glittery emo vamp compared to what we really were faced with.

Count Siva looked to be in his late forties to early fifties. He had salt-and-pepper hair and a full beard and mustache. He was short, fat, and not very evil-looking, actually, Siva reminded me of Dom DeLouis. Siva was decked

out in a white chef's suit with a "Kiss The Cook" apron.

"So I suppose the two of you are here to scare me

away, am I correct?"

"I don't know about the scare," I replied, "but your

neighbors are kinda fed up with your behavior."

"Meaning?"

"Quit eatin' the freakin' natives," said Vinny.

"Speaking of eating, would you gentlemen care for a

bite?"

I cringed at the thought, both by the mental image and

who it potentially could be.

"I'm afraid all I have to offer are some potatoes and

corn."

"No prob, Rob. I've got some food with me," said

Vinny, "If ya like steaks."

Count Siva leveled a smile at Vinny, "I love steak. I

am sorry to say that my cook is away, however."

"Easy enough Fangs, I'll cook them up. Where to?"

"Follow the hallway to the right. Enter the third

door on the left. That is the kitchen, help yourself."

Vinny bowed curtly and left, leaving me alone with the

Count.

"Would you care for a game of chess?"

I nodded that I would and seated myself at the game board. Funny, I don't remember there being a chessboard there a moment ago. I sat on the white side, in a chair made to mimic the white bishop, Siva sat opposite me in a dark chair in the shape of the black knight. The pieces were carved out of marble, with incredible attention to detail.

I opened with my pawn, watched his counter, and set myself on the game. It had been years since I was challenged to chess, and even then I was barely good enough to make it fun. Siva countered, I countered his counter, and so on. Then I had the first opening.

"Check," I said, feeling more confident. Siva had missed my king's bishop with a clear path to his king.

"Did you know that chess originated in the Gupta Empire of India in the 6th century? It is one of the oldest games of strategy and intelligence." He moved his bishop to block mine.

"I see you have studied it, though I must admit to being a true novice." I moved out one of my knights. "I prefer a more violent form of entertainment. Video games being one."

He looked at me, a puzzled expression clouding his face. "You do play well quite well, though."

"Thank you, Count. Though I can't be the toughest opponent you have faced."

"No," he replied, "The toughest opponent was a black unicorn. I would have won too, but he brought beer with him. It took me days to recover, by then I had sworn off that infernal beverage."

"You should have let him teach you a few moves, check and mate."

Siva looked down at the board, sure enough, I had beaten him. He was in the process of asking for a rematch when Vinny entered.

"Come and get it, dinner is ready."

We made our way to the dining room. The table was a large oak number, able to seat twenty-two people. Today it would seat three. Vinny had laid out the entrees and filled our goblets as we sat. For the Count, Vinny had poured win from the cellars. For myself he had poured water, knowing my dislike for alcohol. Vinny filled his own goblet from a flask he had hidden on his person. Not for the first time I swore I didn't want to know where he kept it, or what was in it.

Vinny had cooked six steaks, enough for two each or leftovers for the servants. He had also roasted a dozen ears of corn and had a massive hot skillet of spiced fried potatoes.

I could tell by the first taste of steak that Vinny had cooked it in lots of garlic. We both ate quietly, watching as the Count ate everything except for the steak. When at last we believed he was on to us, the Count sliced off a large chunk of meat and popped it in his mouth.

We anticipated a lot of choking, cursing, maybe even some fire and brimstone. What we got instead was a look of surprise and satisfaction.

"This is wonderful," Siva mumbled between bites.

"You like garlic?" I asked

"Absolutely, it has to be one of the best spices ever. You can put it on almost anything."

When we finished dinner Vinny brought in the dessert. He had prepared a pie, served with a robust coffee. The pie was still quite hot, the apples seasoned lightly. It was the coffee that was our last weapon. Vinny had 'found' some holy water and had made the coffee from it.

The Count finished his pie, sipped at his coffee, and watched us.

"So you gentlemen believe that you could destroy me, in my own home, and with food? You have courage, as no one else has dared enter my castle. At least, not without being on the menu."

The Count stood and stretched, as if sleepy after a heavy meal.

"Unfortunately for you, there will be no returning to town. No death for me. Above all, no rescue for my pets."

Count Siva's face began to shifting, his body grew and distorted, fingernails becoming longer and sharper. He looked like no creature I have ever seen nor read about. Count Siva had become a demonic beast, ready to attack at any moment.

"Look behind you! What's that?" shouted Vinny, pointing behind Siva.

The Count never so much as glanced.

"You mook, that only works in movies!" I yelled.

Quickly I picked up the steak knife resting on my plate. I flipped it over to grasp the tip and threw it towards the demon. It rotated seventy-four times before striking Count Siva in the center of his forehead with the oak handle. He roared out, clasping his head. That gave Vinny and me the moment we needed to escape. Following Vinny, we bolted down the hallway until we reached some stairs.

"Down?" I asked. Vinny shrugged and started down.

"I have a bad feeling about this," I stated. We had walked into a crypt of sorts.

"He had wine stacked down here, along with a phone

booth. Maybe we can call for help."

"Vinny, did you say phone booth?"

"Yep, thought it was weird myself, but look, there it

is."

Sure enough, in the corner was an old, English style

red phone booth. I opened the door and saw an

advertisement over the phone. Being the only number I saw,

I picked up the receiver and dialed. Vinny crammed himself

into the booth with me as the other end rang. The

connection answered in what sounded like a fax or modem

series of tones and static. Colors flashed before us.

When the show ended we were in a new basement.

We opened the booth and started to look around. The

room was filled with wine and cooking stock. There were

stairs in the northern wall near barrels of fresh-looking

vegetables. Carefully we ascended them, ending at a trap

door in the ceiling. Cautiously Vinny opened the door.

The aromatic teasing of fettuccine alfredo and shrimp

parmesan filled the air. We entered the room of heavenly

aromas, our stomachs forgetting we had just eaten. Several

people were seated at tables all around us, Italian food

resting before each patron.

A fairly short thin man walked up to us, dressed in a

fine tuxedo. He wore glasses and had a black beanie on his head that was covering the tips of his ears. On his lapel was a paw print of some sort embroidered.

"Welcome my friends to Tony's Spaghetti Shack. I am Tony."

"We're home," said Vinny

I wished I was so sure.

Chapter 7

Crossroads

In which Vinny makes an offer I could refuse and we make a

revelation

As we expected, we were not home in a time and space
kind of way. This, however, was much better than any other
place we had been since our arrival. Tony set us up with a
room upstairs from his restaurant. We promised to work off
the debt in trade. I knew by experience that Vinny was an
incredibly gifted cook. I offered to play the piano if
Tony could get a hold of one. Tony promised to have one
mailed the next morning.

We must have slept for an eternity. I dreamt that I
was the referee to a wrestling match between a panther and
a demonic chef. The smell of cappuccino woke me. Vinny
was already up, breakfast in hand.

"Good morning, Guido. I got ya some eggs, bacon, and
pancakes. Help yourself."

"Bacon? Thought this place was strictly no on meats."

"Naw, man, that's just in Lycan. Here people stay
people."

I sat at the small table in the corner, Vinny joined

me with the tray. He handed me the coffee, the flavors burst over my neglected tongue.

"Guido, one question for ya. You have years of hand to hand combat training, and considerably talented with knives. You had the skills and moment, so why didn't you kill Siva?"

"One, I doubt it would have stopped him. If he is a true vampire, a simple knife would have no effect other than pissing him off even more."

"And two?"

"I'm not sure. For some reason something made me adjust my throw. I just wanted us to escape, to think things through and find a better way."

Vinny nodded, satisfied with my answer.

"Guido, I'm sorry about the poker game. I got carried away."

"No harm, Vinny. I'm sorry about the steaks."

"It's cool, they were good at least. Hey Guido, do you think she likes me?"

"Who," I asked, feeling a bit of jealousy. "Kitty?"

"Colleen."

"Who?" I asked

"Colleen, the girl from the library. She was downstairs this morning for breakfast. She said she always comes here whenever she goes to the post office. Did you

know her hobby is restoring ancient books and paintings?"

"I guess she thinks that is fun?"

"She is so cool. Smart too."

"Think you could fall in love with a bird?"

"Couldn't be different than you falling for a cat."

I blushed a bit. Vinny's grin told too many tales.

"I thought you were sleeping."

"And I thought you would enjoy the privacy."

I smiled, remembering that night.

"Well Vin-man, let's get going. We have a lot of work

to do if we expect to save our fair maidens."

A loud crash followed by yells and curses came from

downstairs. Vinny and I ran down the stairway, expecting

to see the Count waiting for us. Instead, we found Tony

smacking around a familiar person with a serving tray.

"Vinny, it's him again, that Mark guy!"

Vinny grabbed Tony from behind, trying to calm the

situation.

"Lemme go! I'm gonna break his nose, then his ears.

Then I'm gonna pluck out his eyelashes and poke him in the

eyes. His bottom lip I'm gonna pull up over his head and

tie it to his underwear!"

"Calm, Tony. Calm yourself." Vinny added pressure

with his hands. His arms had snaked around Tony's, pulling them back towards Vinny. Vinny's hands were clenched together, keeping Tony from using his arms.

"Now what happened?" asked Vinny when he felt Tony relax.

"That idiot was trying to poison my customers. I hired him this morning when he said he was a great waiter. Then I find him poisoning my patrons!"

"Poison? I'll have you know that Peef is not poisonous. It is all-natural, maybe a bit salty, but not at all poisonous."

"Peef?" I asked. "What is Peef?"

Vinny shook his head, "Guido, give it a rest bro. Tony, go take a smoke break, I'll handle him from here."

"You realize, of course, he's fired. Just get his ass out of my place."

Vinny released Tony, pointing towards the kitchen. Tony gave a final glare at Mark and walked through the kitchen doors. Vinny turned towards the former waiter.

"So what's your name anyway? Is it Mark or Ken?"

The waiter burst into tears, crying out, "I don't even know! I can't remember!"

"Vinny, just kick him out, be done with him."

"Naw man, I wanna keep him. He's kinda like a lost

mutt."

"Dude, the guy doesn't have a name or a brain for that matter. I bet you could count his brain cells on his hand and still be able to give the finger to the Count."

"I think I'll call him Luigi...that sounds like a good sidekick name."

"Luigi, the Pope?" asked our new friend. It brought back memories to me of the first time we saw him working in the Rosary.

"Sure, now do us a favor and go clean our room out. We'll let you join us so long as you work for it."

Luigi charged off and up the stairs. I stared at Vinny.

"Vinny...why?"

"Cannon fodder, vampire snacks. I'm just kidding," he quickly added, seeing my shocked expression. "He's from the area, he'll be a great help, I just know it."

"Just don't kill him like you did the hamster."

Vinny grinned at me. I know many girls who have fallen for that grin. Luckily it had no effect on me. I knew he was up to something.

"Come on Vinny, let's check out the town. We still need to find out how far we are from Lycan."

Hoping that Luigi will be safe in the room, Vinny and

I stepped outside. We had both expected to see another bustling city like Cheshire. We were surprised to see nothing of the sort. All there was to see were two buildings and two roads that intersected.

Across the streets, exactly opposite of where Tony's was, there sat a post office. The building was fairly large, but no windows could be seen. The only portal of any form was the door in the front.

We approached the door, curious as to what we would find. A sign on the door read, "Welcome to Crossroads." Shrugging, I opened the door and entered with Vinny right behind. The room before us was large and very bright. There were velvet rope barriers set up to help form lines, yet no one was here.

Advertisements adorned the walls, pictures of exotic places, and people appeared to be waving and calling us. We entered the queue line and wandered our way to the counter. When we finally arrived my growing suspicion was confirmed.

A small, fat man waited for us. He had a long white beard, a red coat trimmed in white, and small square glasses. He smiled as he looked up at us.

"Bout time you showed up, I've been waiting for you for a week now."

"How could you be waiting for us," I asked, "if we didn't arrive until today?"

"Aren't you boys the ones I sent to England last week?"

"Nope, must have us confused with some other mooks," commented Vinny.

"Oops, I see," said the Postmaster. "Forget I said anything. How can I help you fine gents?"

"A few days ago," I began, "you delivered a book to my friend and me."

"Possible, I deliver lots of things."

"This was a book in a brown box. I book about time travel. This book brought us to this world."

"Ah yes, that reminds me. It was delivered to the wrong person. The intended person was Prince Machiavelli. Any chance, do you have it with you?"

"Sorry, but no. Question, who sent out the book?"

"Well, usually I am not supposed to say, but if you could give her the book then everything would be righted."

"Her? Who?"

"Let me see here," he replied, checking his ledgers, "Kitty of Lycan."

I try to hide my surprise, Vinny did a much better job of it.

"Thank you...err"

"Call me Nicholas."

"Of course, Nicholas. Thank you, we'll be back."

"Oh, I know," he replied, "But please try to remember return postage."

I looked at him quizzically, Vinny pulled me out of the post office. We made our way back to Tony's relieved to find Luigi still in the room. Vinny took Luigi aside and whispered in his ear. I couldn't make out a word, but it had to be good as Luigi swept Vinny into a great hug and became all smiles. I was afraid that Vinny may start breaking kneecaps for such an action, but Vinny just chuckled.

"Ok," I said as Luigi left, "what was that all about?"

"I sent him on a mission, keeps him out of our way for a while. So, you ready to go?"

"For what?"

"I assume you want to go back to Lycan to talk to Kitty."

I nodded, the thought had crossed my mind.

"I have a better idea," I said. "That book was mailed through space and time to reach us. Did you see the advertisements on the wall? I think people can be mailed also."

"And just what kind of a trip would we take? You
still thinking of running back for the home?"

"Nope, better. If you read your vampire history and
watch the good movies, you would know that Dr. Van Helsing
was the greatest vampire hunter in history."

"Hey, Guido, lay off my brownies. Helsing was
fictional."

"Back to those adverts on the wall, one of them was
for a vacation to Pern. Another was offering tickets to a
Quidditch game. If a person can visit a fictional place,
why not have a fictional person come here?"

"Seems like a physics question, could a fictional
person really exist in the real world?"

"You're here, Vinny."

"Good point, when do we leave?"

I grinned, "Now is good."

Chapter 8

2 Males 2 Mail

In which we visit a Doctor in need of a doctor.

"Can I help you?" asked the Postmaster.

"Yep, we need to mail a package somewhere and we aren't really sure as to how to do it."

"All mail must be sent with an official Crossroads-supplied courier box. The address must be clearly written. Proper postage is required, however, return postage is free. Will there be any return post?"

"Actually yes, but not for a day or two."

"Simply print "Return to Sender" under the original address. You can call for a pickup from any local phone, if one is not available you can rent a pager from this office."

"Sending fee would be set by weight. The return fee is applicable if you are returning with more weight than what you left with. I would suggest using the restroom before returning. If you are ready, please step up to the scales."

Vinny and I complied, first I stepped up, then I got off and Vinny stepped up. Nicholas waved at me so I stepped back up and Vinny stepped down. A few more times of this went on until Nicholas picked up Vinny and stood him on the scale next to me and glared at me. Together we weighed in at just a little over four hundred pounds.

"The sending fee comes to four hundred gold. I assume you gentlemen carry gold?"

I was about to protest when Vinny opened his jacket.

"Will this do?" Vinny asked as he pulled out a piece of paper. Inscribed upon it was "Chummer's Bum."

"Vinny, what the hell is that?"

"Dude, it is the deed to the bar in Lycan. I won it in a card game the first night we were there. I renamed it and made the former owner the new manager. We'll use it as collateral until we get back."

"When did you have time to do all this?"

"Dude, you don't really think I sleep all the time, do you?"

While we had been talking Nicholas had brought out a large box. It looked more like a cardboard closet than any box I had ever used for shipping.

"Gents, if you could please write the address on the outside and step in."

Vinny stepped up, handed over the deed, and wrote "Doctor Van Helsing, Jolly Old England" on the side.

"I hope this works," I muttered as I followed him in.

The sides closed in, the lid fwapped shut above us, darkening the interior. The was barely enough room for the both of us to fit. We never did ask how long the trip would take, our answer came less than a minute later as the box opened around us.

I had expected to see the postmaster, but we got a different shock. We were there, in England. However, from the looks of things, this England was neither jolly nor old.

A man was looking at us, or actually, past us. To be honest it didn't look like he could focus at all. He was about six foot, dressed all in silver. He had flowing white hair and bloodshot eyes. In his right hand was a television remote, in the left was a plastic bottle of cheap rum.

"What are you, I distinctively remem...rememem...I bought a girl. You don't look like a girl. You don't smell like a girl. What's your name, madam?"

"Guido, may I?" asked Vinny.

I was about to give Vinny the okay to thrash this drunk any way he wanted, but before I could say anything, we were interrupted. The plate-glass windows behind Helsing shattered. The whipping wind tore through me, suffocating me with a cold blast. Vinny and I scrambled

away from the box, ran out of the room, down the hall, and

ducked into the first room. Helsing followed us in.

"What in the nine levels of hell was that thing?" I

screamed at him, barely holding my terror in check over

what I had just seen come through the window.

"That was the Prince."

"Prince?" I asked, "What Prince?"

"He has been following me for years. My great, great

grandfather killed his kind, he wants revenge."

"He who?" asked Vinny.

"He goes by the name of Vrolok. He is the self-

proclaimed Malkavian Prince. If you ask me, he's nuts."

"But no one asked you," came a quiet but calm voice.

"It is time Petre, time for you to pay the price of what

your ancestors did."

Standing before us was the Prince known as Vrolok. He

towered over us at well over six feet tall. His jet black

hair draped over his shoulders, contrasting with his very

pale skin. His gleaming blue eyes shown easily in the

darkness of the room, as did his very sharp teeth. This

was a true vampire in all its glory.

"Quick Van Helsing, slay it" I shouted.

Vrolok laughed, light and charming yet mixed with a

deadly edge.

"Van Helsing is nothing more than a lazy drunk. If I were a bottle of scotch I would worry about being destroyed by him."

"Guido, quick, the phone! Call the Postmaster and get us the hell out of here!"

I grabbed the phone off the stand and dialed "777."

Vrolok dove towards us, Vinny jumped forward to defend. Vrolok crouched into a classic martial arts stance.

"I know Iron Butterfly," said the vampire.

"I love that band!" Shouted Vinny, striking an air guitar pose.

Vrolok swooped upon us, lunging with kicks and punches. Vinny simply sidestepped and fired off a left hook. It connected with the side of Vrolok's jaw, dropping the vampire into a motionless form.

"How the hell did you do that?" I asked.

Vinny opened his left hand revealing a rosary.

"Where did you get that from?"

"Found it."

"Where?"

"Sister Mother Mary Catherine something or other…"

"Got ya, you 'found' it."

"Ok, can we leave now before he wakes up?"

We dragged the crying Van Helsing to the box, closing the lid behind us. We felt a jolt, and then the lid reopened. We were back at the Post Office.

"What took you fellows so long? I've been waiting a week for you to return."

"Sorry dude," said Vinny, "We had a run-in with the local crazies, even brought one of them back with us."

As Vinny was explaining what had happened and attempted to settle up our debt, I pondered by what the Postmaster meant by a week.

CHAPTER 9

Count On It

In which we pay our second visit to the first vampire.

Count Siva entered his study. His candles flickered in acknowledgment of his arrival. He was pleased with himself. When his spy reported that the two strangers were gone, Siva had launched an immediate attack. He now had twenty of the villagers in his dungeon. It took him an entire week, but now he had enough to last through winter.

"Master," whispered a voice, "Master, they have returned. They are standing outside as we speak."

"Let them in. It is time I dealt with these fools."

Count Siva left the room. His spy transformed into a human. She smiled out the window as she looked down at Vinny and Guido.

"Soon, very soon. You thought you could love me. Now you will learn the full truth."

A storm rumbled over the castle of Count Siva. No servants greeted us or opened the doors. Nervously the three of us entered. I led the way, carrying a torch to light the way. Vinny followed, his rosary wrapped around his left hand. Petre Van Helsing followed, or rather stumbled and staggered behind us.

We were glad to be out of the rain. The cold, however, seemed to decide to join us. We made our way to the library. No fire warmed us. It appeared that the place was empty. I heard a scream behind me, spinning around I caught a glimpse of something rapidly dragging Petre away.

"Dude, what the hell was that?"

"No clue," I replied, "but it is getting away!"

We raced out of the room, a door at the end of the hallway shut quickly. We ran towards the door but found it locked. Vinny ran back to the library and returned a moment later, a letter opener in hand. It took Vinny a few seconds to pop the lock.

We threw open the door and charged into the darkness. My torch blowing out as we entered. The door clicked shut behind me.

I fumbled around, trying to find the door. I heard another door open and close, yet no light was shown. Panic began to set in when suddenly a fire flared at the end of the room. I was standing, very much alone, in the dining room. There was no sign of Vinny.

I found the second door, tried it, and found it easy to open. It revealed a small corridor, ending at a spiral staircase leading up. At the top was another door, this one painted red. I entered it quietly.

The room was small, occupied by a writing desk, a small bed, and a woman.

"About time, you were worrying me."

Shocked by who I saw, I never saw her draw the knife.

Chapter 10

Petre's

In which a part of the plan is set.

Petre woke, aching, suffering, but still alive. He had felt this way before. There had been countless mornings after an all-night binge. This was the worse, he had no alcohol to chase the pains away.

For twenty years Petre had been hiding, running from vampires. Now he was given the chance to redeem himself. All he had to show for it was getting captured.

Slowly Petre rose, brushed off the straw and dirt from his clothes, and looked around. Through the darkness, he could make out stables. The smell of horses assailed him. He sneezed violently.

A laugh echoed around him. From the darkness came a beast. A large wolfhound with matted brown fur. It strode towards Van Helsing. The horses in the stable circled nervously.

Petre backed away from the wolfhound. With every step Petre made, the hound grew closer. Something sharp poked Petre, causing him to jump in alarm. He reached back, wrapping his fingers around the wooden handle. Quickly he brought his find in front of him.

The Wolfhound stopped, eyeing the pitchfork cautiously. Petre stepped forward, the wolfhound retreated a few steps. His confidence grew. Petre charged the wolfhound, chasing it until it charged up the steps and into the loft.

Victoriously, Petre turned to escape. A hand snatched the pitchfork from behind. Petre felt the hard shove that landed him against a beam. The wolfhound had morphed, became more manlike than canine. The wolf-like beast bent over, morphing again.

Slowly the fur receded. The claws drew back. Count Siva rose, flexing his arms. Smiling, Siva regarded the weapon and his captive.

"The hunter of vampires. This is what history says of your famous ancestor. I have read his books, you should be very proud of him. Sad that the same cannot be said of you."

"If I have regrets, it is that I will miss watching your kind be destroyed."

"My kind? You know nothing of 'my kind.'"

"I do," came a voice from behind.

Siva wheeled around, Luigi stood before him. Moonlight glinted off Luigi's armor. The symbol of a king bearing a cross in the left hand and a rose in the right is shown upon his breastplate.

"And who are you?" asked Siva.

"I am Luigi the Pope. I am the spiritual leader for Vinny and Guido. I am the official carver of the sacred Mashed Potatoes and the designer of peef. I am an artist."

"Anything else?"

"I know Santa Clause."

"Can you catch?"

Siva hurled the pitchfork at Luigi. Petre took the moment of distraction and ran for the doorway, disappearing into the night. The pitchfork arched towards Luigi, who simply closed his eyes, his lips moving silently.

The pitchfork thudded loudly. Luigi would have been killed, had he not vanished a split second earlier. All that was left was his gilded cape lying on the floor. Count Siva approached cautiously. He tapped at the cape with his foot. Satisfied he turned to deal with Petre.

"Damn," he whispered

Chapter 11

Vinny Da Mac

In which Vinny is in a jail…again…nothing new here folks.

Vinny woke but did not move. He kept his eyes closed, assessing the situation. He could smell stale sweat and urine. He could hear the distant jingling of keys on a key ring as someone paced. He realized he was lying on his back on cold, damp rocks.

Vinny slowly opened his eyes, allowing them to adjust to the darkness. He saw that he was in jail of some sort. The floor has straw scattered about. Along the walls were sets of chains. Thankfully he wasn't in them.

He heard the jingling again. A guard was heading his way. Vinny moved towards the back of the cell. He had no weapons available. Even his rosary was taken. It didn't matter, Vinny had a plan.

As the guard was passing, Vinny let out a cry.

"Whatsa matta? You zick?" asked the guard. He unlocked the door and entered the cell. "Masta wants ya good. Not zick, so youse betta be playin." The guard crouched over Vinny.

"I am playin," said Vinny, popping the guard with a

quick jab, jumped to his feet and followed it with a left
hook. Vinny pulled the unconscious guard to the darkest
corner and went to work covering him up with the straw.
Vinny then relieved the guard of his keys.

"Dude! My beautiful suit was ruined!" cried Vinny,
giving the guard one last kick to the rear.

Vinny locked the cell behind him and scanned for an
exit. There were several more cells around him. In each
were different animals. Vinny unlocked the nearest cell.
The animals inside transforming as he freed them. Within a
few minutes, Vinny had freed all of the villagers.

Vinny found the stairs and led the former captives up
to the main doors. The villagers fled past him, several
changing back into their animal forms. Many shouted out
thanks to Vinny on their way out.

"Okay Mr. Sharpteeth, your turn to be Vinned."

Vinny ran back down the hallways, nearly running over
Luigi in the process.

"Hey Luigi, you made it!"

"Mr. Vinny, I brought what you asked for."

"Let's get to the cellar then," Vinny said with a
grin.

Chapter 12

Guido da Knife

In which my heart is nearly pierced but fully crushed.

I grasped at the knife, desperate yet futile. The six-inch blade had passed into my chest. The heat was unbearable, yet I knew it would soon pass. Funny, I had studied martial arts all my life. I was a trained knife fighter, yet this was the first time that I had been on the receiving end.

I sat against the desk, unable or unwilling to remove the dagger. Standing over me was our traitor. She watched me, no remorse in her eyes. She was waiting I knew, waiting for my death.

I tried to speak, no words would come out. I was having trouble breathing.

"Problem, my love?" asked Kitty. "Please, feel free to tell me how it feels. Does it hurt more to have that dagger thrust into you, or seeing me do it?"

"Why?" was all I could manage.

"The Count is a very persuasive man. When he arrived years ago, I knew I was in love. He courted me for months. Then one night we consummated our love. The passion stirred new urges, that night we hunted together, feasting on meat as beasts were meant to. I bet you still believe he is a vampire."

I willed myself to stand. Intense pain shot through me, staggering me. I yanked the dagger out, my hand slippery with my own blood.

"I have been watching you, daily in fact. I admit I like your style. Too bad you opposed us."

"You still," I whispered, "still can't…"

"Win? Already have. Siva is dealing with the 'vampire hunter.' Your friend Vinny is locked away. You are all alone."

"Wrong!" came a throaty growl. Kitty spun towards the voice, pitching backward as a black panther slammed into her.

"Run!" growled the panther.

I focused all my energy on escaping. I fell more than ran down the stairs. Strong hands caught me, dragging me away. I was too weak to fight, instead, I tried to simply focus on who held me.

My rescuer sat me in a chair. We were in the dining room. I realized that it was Petre who was tending to me. He pressed fine linen napkins against my wound and used a torn piece of a tablecloth to bind the napkins.

I was about to thank him when Siva entered.

Chapter 14

Reunion

In which my death comes too soon.

"So this is where you ran off to, Petre. So naughty of you to run away. Now, like your friend here, it is time for you to die."

"Allow me," said Kitty, joining us.

"Wait, my love. Come here first."

Kitty did as she was commanded, stopping next to the Count. Siva drew back her long hair, revealing a scar on her neck. Please, Siva let go of her hair.

"My love," said Siva, "He is yours to kill."

Kitty launched herself at Petre. He didn't have the quickness to escape, nor the knowledge of self-defense. He was overpowered quickly. Kitty stood from the crumpled mass.

"Pity, his neck snapped. These humans are so fragile."

"What of the other one, the stupid friend of his?"

Kitty smiled, "Locked away, as you commanded. Shall we celebrate our victory?" She picked up two glasses from the table. A swirling yellow liquid inside each.

"What is it?" asked Siva.

"Amontillado, two hundred years old."

"I have heard of it, read about it in a book once. Yet I have never tasted it."

"Then by all means my lord."

Count Siva downed the drink in one tilt. His face contorted in agony. He glared fiercely at Kitty, who just stood there smiling. She poured out her glass onto the floor. Count Siva clutched at his throat, collapsing to the floor.

From the side door, Vinny and Luigi entered. He walked over to the Count, holding a vial in his hand.

"I'll make you a deal. A life for a life. You save Guido, I save you."

Count Siva nodded weakly. Darkness descended upon me.

Chapter 15

All Weird Things…

In which loose ends are tied and answers are presented.

I awoke, not quite sure how long I was out. I was in bed. Vinny, Luigi, Kitty, Colleen, and Count Siva were with me. I shot up quickly, well tried to. Vinny's hand grabbed my shoulder and eased me back down.

"Easy man," Vinny said. "It's okay. Everything is cool."

"Explain."

"I can," replied Count Siva. "I came to this land as a child. My parents raised me in the castle. What Colleen told you was true."

"Colleen?"

"I am sorry," Colleen said quietly. "I made myself look like Kitty. I knew it would make you an easier target when the time came."

"Colleen and I share a rare ability," said Siva. "We can shift our own natural features, as well as the type of animal we are. Our daughter has the same ability, as we learned earlier tonight."

"That was you in the dining room," I said to Kitty.

"You were also the panther upstairs. Somehow, I knew."

Kitty smiled at this.

"Count Siva is my father, my real father. I found out about his truth in a book at the library."

"Quick question, who was it that night-"

"Me," said Kitty quickly, blushing.

"So where do we stand?"

"I made a bargain," answered Siva. "I saved your life in exchange for the antidote to the poison. I have also agreed to banishment from this place. Colleen and I will leave as soon as Petre returns."

"Where is Petre?" I asked.

"At the post office," said Vinny. "He's getting the box ready for their trip."

"I'm back," we heard from the doorway.

"Good to see ya alive," I said.

"Thanks to your friends. I ran into Vinny and Kitty before Siva found you. I knew what Vinny had planned."

"Vinny?" I asked, astonished.

"Yep."

"Okay Siva, Colleen, time to go."

Siva and Colleen entered the postal box, Petre joined them.

"Where are you going?"

"With them," replied Petre. "I'm taking them back to my world. I have a friend who just loves competition. With Siva on my side, maybe I can finally give him some back."

I smiled, knowing that Petre had a strong ally to help him.

Vinny closed the lid, the box vanished.

"All right, what was this poison that Siva drank?"

"Peef," said Luigi.

"And what the hell is peef?"

"Beef flavored urine product," said Luigi.

"That's nasty!"

"Dude," said Vinny, "I told you never to ask."

"So what was the antidote?"

Luigi chuckled, "Water."

"So now what do we do?" asked Vinny.

"I know," said Luigi. "This letter came for you. It's an offer for the employment of your services."

Luigi handed me the letter, I read it and started smiling at what I saw.

"Vinny, feel like staying?"

"No problem, Guido. Like I want to go back to a world with the IRS."

I shivered at the thought.

"Okay, so how about we work up a deal to stay here.
We'll make this our office."

"The spaghetti joint?" asked Kitty.

Vinny grinned, "Works for me."

"So what do we call our little enterprise? Vinny and
Guido's Detective Agency?"

"Nope," said Luigi. "How about we just call ourselves
Mooks."

"I like it," I said. "Now what about Tony?"

"He's fine with it," said Luigi. "I asked him about
it when the letter arrived yesterday."

"How did you know what was going to happen?"

"Santa told me."

"Luigi," I said. "How about I make you in charge of
acquisitions."

"Can I still be the Pope?"

"Yep," replied Vinny.

"So where next?" asked Kitty. I smiled up at her.

"Tonight, the other two are going out to celebrate.
You and I are staying in."

"And then," said Vinny.

"And then it's none of your business."

"And then," said Luigi.

"And then what?" I asked.

"And then we take the new job," said both Vinny and Luigi.

I grinned at them. Let the games begin, I thought to myself.

Afterword

    Vinny walked up to the door for the third time that
weekend. The symbol was still there, glowing in that deep
blue. Frustrated he walked off, deciding he needed a good
poker game.

The End